Courage Hats

WRITTEN BY **Kate Hoefler**   ILLUSTRATED BY **Jessixa Bagley**

chronicle books · san francisco

Not everyone loves a train.
That's the world.

For all the Maes and Bears
in this world. —K. H.

For Taylor. —J. B.

Text copyright © 2022 by Kate Hoefler.
Illustrations copyright © 2022 by Jessixa Bagley.
All rights reserved. No part of this book may
be reproduced in any form without written
permission from the publisher.

Library of Congress Cataloging-in-
Publication Data available.

ISBN 978-1-7972-0276-1

Manufactured in China.

Design by Lydia Ortiz.
Typeset in Recoleta and Brandon Grotesque.
The illustrations in this book were
rendered in graphite and watercolor.

10 9 8 7 6 5 4 3 2 1

Chronicle Books LLC
680 Second Street
San Francisco, California 94107

Chronicle Books—we see things differently.
Become part of our community at
www.chroniclekids.com.

But sometimes,
you have to take one anyway.

For Mae, the train went deep into bear places.
A bear was big and ate small things.
And Mae was small.

For Bear, the train went deep into people places.
A person was small and ate big things.
And Bear was big.

Courage is something that comes from your heart—
but if you can't find it there,

you can wear it
on your head at first.

Mae wore a special hat
so a bear would think
she was just another bear.

Bear wore a special hat
so a person would think
he was just another person.

But it takes awhile
for a heart to
catch up to a hat.

So Mae found a
big grown-up to sit with.

And Bear found a
small cub to sit with.

Honey in your tea?
Mae asked the grown-up.

Thank you, Bear said to the cub.
And off they went.

No matter how you feel about a train,
someone else feels the same way.

You're lucky if that someone has a blanket and snack.

There was a lot to notice, too.

Especially the big things they could have missed:
How a train carries the sky on its back.
How birds join it.

How to make a friend
who also thinks
this feels like flying.

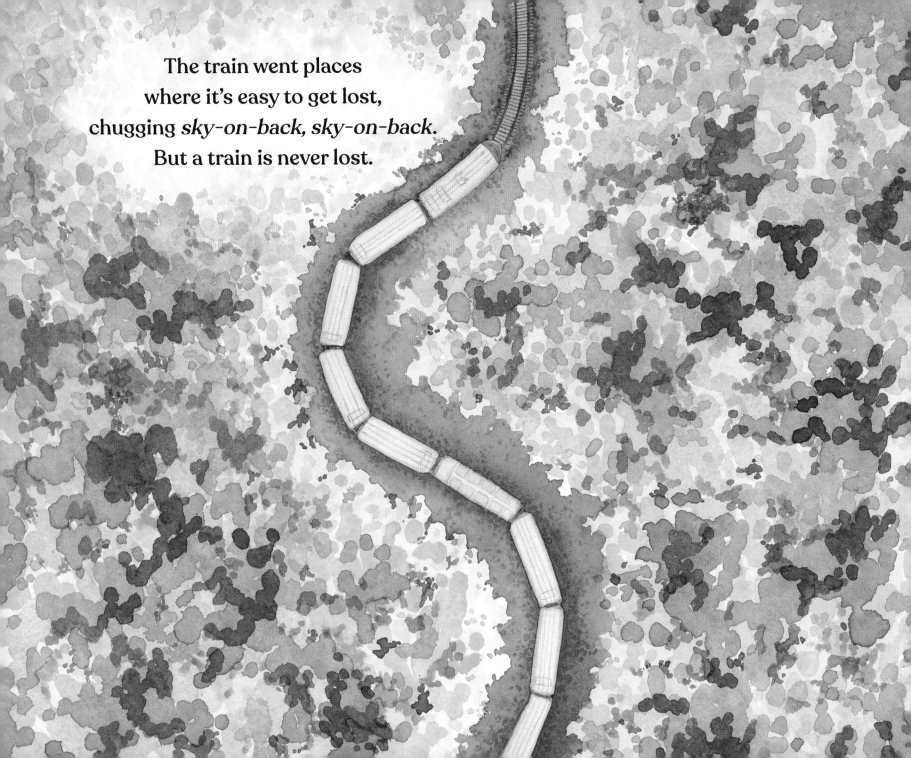

The train went places
where it's easy to get lost,
chugging *sky-on-back, sky-on-back.*
But a train is never lost.

And they began to feel less lost on it.

When the train went deep,
deep in the woods,
Mae wondered if she might
find herself near bears.
I'm glad you're with me,
she said to the grown-up.

Because she'd never been so deep
in a bear place.

Without the grown-up, she might have missed
what was right next to her.

And when the train went deep,
deep in the city,
Bear wondered if he might
find himself near people.
I'm glad you're with me,
he said to the small cub.

Because he had never been so deep
in a people place.

Without the cub, he might have missed
what was right next to him.

Because not everyone loves a train.

That's the world.

There may be bears.
There may be people.

But the friend you make in a deep place
is an important friend.

There may be bears.
There may be people.

But the friend you make in a deep place
is an important friend.

So important that when the trip is over, you give each other something special.

A hat.

And when you take your hat off,
someone else will, too.

That, too, is the world.